D0943442

The Great Whale Star

Toria Hungerford

ISBN-13: 978-0-578-43909-9

DEDICATED TO MY HUSBAND THOMAS,
my soul mate, who fills my life with love, laughter, and magic.
Our love is a thread of stars interwoven into the fabric of the universe.
An eternity of lifetimes together await us!

♥

CONTENTS

"The sea, once it casts its spell,
holds one in its net of wonder forever."

~Jacques Yves Cousteau

TORIA HUNGERFORD

ACKNOWLEDGMENTS

To my mother, the first person to ever read this little book,
and to my family and friends who encouraged me along the way,
I am grateful.

Celeste, Koa, Ollie, Mya, Hewa and I, would like to thank my illustrator Aaron Herrera for
his amazing artistic talent, and my editor John Fox.

A special thank you to my two creative muses who inspire me daily:
my loving husband, Thomas
and Grandmother Moon.

☽

TORIA HUNGERFORD

CHAPTER 1

ARE THEY HERE YET?

Celeste woke to the sound of the gentle waves lapping around her and within seconds she swam to her mother's side asking, "Mama, where's Mya? Are they here yet? Where are they?"

Her mother, Naomi, was gathering seaweed with the dolphin elders in preparation for the upcoming welcome ceremony. She greeted Celeste with a warm smile, and spoke calmly, "Settle down Celeste...no, they're not here yet. Now that you're awake, I'll need your help with collecting coral, braiding seaweed and..."

Celeste tuned out her mother's voice and stared up at the deep purple, blue, and pink sky, which to her looked like a giant floating pearl in the sky.

"...and as soon as you're done with that, I'll have you help your grandmother."

"What? I didn't hear you mom," Celeste dunked her head in and out of the water while blowing bubbles. "What'd you say? Can't hear you...can't hear you."

"Celeste! Stop clowning around and get busy with—" But before her mother could finish her sentence, Celeste had dunked below the surface, leaving nothing but air bubbles.

"Celeste!" her mother yelled, "Celeste! Get back here!" her mother ordered, as she turned to the dolphin elders and grinned with embarrassment. They pretended not to notice.

Celeste could hear her mother's call but deliberately ignored her. She swam away as quickly as she could, knowing her mother was too busy to chase her.

The truth was, she was frustrated! She had waited all summer long for her best friend Mya, the youngest of the sea giants, to return home. The sea giants were the humpback whales of the island and had left in the spring for their annual migration to Alaska. Since summer was over, they had begun their long journey back home to the tropical island of Ka La'ume Bay and Celeste was tired of waiting.

Celeste swam close to the shore and watched the people of the village carrying baskets of purple pearls on shore and crushing them into large bowls. She looked up to the highest cliff and noticed the chief of the island standing at the top, tossing purple dust into the clouds. For a split second she wondered what he was doing, but her thoughts were interrupted by a school of fish that swam by and she took off chasing them.

She chased the fish through the red forest of tall kelp and passed the colorful coral reefs. She ventured out further and further until finally, she realized she had reached the sunken old sea ship that her mother had always told her to stay away from. It had a huge hole on its side and was covered with algae. Her mother warned it was a favorite hangout of sharks and eels, too dangerous for a young dolphin. But she ignored her mother's warning and stuck her head inside the giant hole to take a quick peek. It was dark and scary inside the belly of the ship. She couldn't see much.

"Hellllooooo!" she shouted, and heard her voice echo back, "*hello, hello, hello…*" She giggled.

Then she heard, "Stay out!" in a deep, scary voice. Terrified, she turned to flee, but a giant current pushed her straight into the hole of the ship! She tossed and turned, and flipped and spun. When she caught her balance, she found herself in the belly of the ship, completely surrounded by darkness!

"Get out!" the voice grumbled louder. Celeste scrambled as fast as she could towards the exit.

Suddenly the idea of helping her mother prepare for the ceremony sounded *really* good to her. She could see the coral reefs in the distance and swam quickly towards them.

Then *SWOOSH*, a large school of fish swam across her path and tossed her behind the coral reefs. She was safe! She cautiously peeked above the coral reefs and watched the fish swim towards the abandoned ship.

"No, no, no! Don't go in there," she shouted. "Over here!"

She could hear several of the fish cry, "Help! Help!" as they darted in several directions. Then she saw a brown sock-like serpent tailing fast behind them, snapping his jaws like a shark. It was the ugliest eel she had ever seen! He chased the fish around the deck of the ship, slamming and chomping into everything that came into his path.

One by one they swam straight into the hole on the side of the ship! They're doomed, she thought. She watched the eel circle the hole on the side of the ship, hesitant to go in. She had to do something to distract him.

"Hey ugly!" Celeste yelled to the eel, not thinking about the consequences. With a crazed look of his red, beady eyes, he stopped in his tracks and swam towards Celeste! His mouth was wide open, and she could see a hundred jagged teeth that reached to the back of his throat, coming straight for her.

As he slithered his way towards her, the eel grumbled, "Mmmm…tasty young dolphin, my favorite!"

CHAPTER 2

THE KALANI PEARL

Celeste shuddered at first when she saw him approaching, but then something inside her ignited, and instinctively, she smacked him hard with her tail. He went sailing across the water and slammed straight into an upside-down wooden crate. The crate flipped over and over, churning up sand into a giant cloud. The eel shook off the blow, and slowly circled back towards her. She could hear a low chuckle that gurgled through his teeth. He was ready for round two.

As the cloud of sand settled, something below caught Celeste's eye. Where the wooden crate had once nestled, she saw something shiny and purple. She glanced back up to see the eel coming towards her. She stared into the dark cave of his mouth filled with yellow, snarled, snapping teeth and her heart pounded. She froze. *Do something, quick!* But there wasn't enough time.

Just then, a red ghost-like blob sideswiped the eel, pushing him out of Celeste's path. It was a giant octopus, and it wrapped its long arms around the eel and squeezed tight. The eel flipped and twisted trying to escape the grasp of the octopus' strong tentacles. The eel snapped his venomous mouth like an alligator, until finally, to avoid getting bit, the octopus released his tight grasp. Celeste sprang into action, and with all her might she smacked the eel with her tail again! The eel went flying over the wooden crate and landed into a pile of what looked like gold nuggets, gemstones, and a beautiful purple pearl.

The octopus stretched out his arms and floated towards the eel like an enormous ghost. The eel swam away defeated, glancing back with his beady eyes.

The octopus shifted his bright, golden eyes to Celeste, drifting slowly back towards her. Celeste trembled at the enormity of the red creature, as he hovered over her.

"Way to go, kid. Mighty punch you got in that tail of yours."

She gulped, "Thanks for coming to my rescue."

"You're mighty welcome. But what were you thinking, picking a fight with Hewa?"

"Hewa?"

"Yes, he's the worst of his kind. Vicious appetite, that one."

"I-I wasn't picking a fight with him. I was just trying to help."

"Well, you could have gotten yourself hurt. Mark my words, he'll be back."

"Really?" Celeste quivered.

"I'm willing to bet," he looked around suspiciously, then held up a gigantic purple pearl with one of his dangly tentacles, "if he happened to see this beauty, the Kalani Pearl!"

Celeste gasped as she gazed at it, "Ohhh…it's so beautiful!"

His eyes shifted to the right, "It's not safe here." He reached across Celeste grabbed the wooden crate and slammed it on the ocean floor. She watched him swiftly place the purple pearl, gold nuggets and jewels into the crate.

He carried the crate as he glided towards the abandoned ship and glanced back, "You comin' kid?"

"Where? Oh no, y-you're not going in there, are you?" Celeste quivered.

"I need to find a new hiding place for the pearl. This seems good enough to me."

"It's dangerous in there," Celeste warned him.

"Where's your sense of adventure, kid?"

"Trust me. There's a ghost, or something in there. It's not safe." She followed him but stopped outside the hole of the ship.

"Ha! A ghost? Good! Sounds like a perfect place to hide the Kalani Pearl." The octopus entered the hole.

CHAPTER 3

THE KEEPER

Celeste waited outside the hole of the ship, waiting for what, she did not know. A scream perhaps? But she heard nothing. Being the curious dolphin that she was, she had to look, she couldn't help it. She poked her head in expecting to see complete darkness like the first time, but instead, blue lights glowed from above, lighting up the entire belly of the ship. Where were the lights coming from? And why weren't they there before?

"Lantern fish," the octopus mumbled. Celeste couldn't see him anywhere! She noticed the crate was placed in the middle of the floor, but where was the octopus?

"What did you say?" she asked loudly, and her voice echoed back, "*What did you say?*"

"Talk quieter," the octopus whispered. "It makes less echo. I said, lantern fish. The little fishes, hovering from the ceiling. That's what they do. They light up dark places."

"Ohhh," she whispered as she peeked up at the fish.

"You going to come in? Or are you going to float outside my front door all day?"

"*This* is your home?" she asked with surprise.

"Home sweet home," he replied.

"So that was you earlier, telling me to get out?"

"Oh, yeah. Sorry about that kid."

She swam along the walls as she looked around. The walls were covered in bright colorful algae that glistened in the light and reminded her of all the colors in the coral reef. There was a garden of red, green, and gold seaweed kelp growing from the floor. It was quite beautiful, and not as scary as she remembered it the first time.

"Where are you?" she asked.

Suddenly, he appeared before her eyes. He sat on top of the crate, with his eight tentacles wrapped around it. Celeste was amazed.

He stretched out one of his eight tentacles in front of her to greet her, "I'm Oliver, but everyone just calls me Ollie. I'm the Keeper of the Kalani Pearl."

"Hi. Uh, my name is Celeste." She offered him her fin. "How did you disappear like that?"

"I'm an octopus… a magician of the sea."

"A magician?"

"That's right kid. That's why I've been selected eight years in a row as the Keeper of the Kalani Pearl." His entire body changed to a deep red color, then to a pale white color, then he disappeared again within a few seconds. She could hear him laughing but only saw bubbles burst from his invisible air funnel.

She giggled, "Cool trick, Ollie. Who are you keeping the Kalani Pearl for?"

"Koa, of course."

Celeste had never heard of Koa and gave an empty stare.

"*Koa.* You know, the Great Whale Star."

"Oh yea…right. Kilo."

"Koa." Ollie turned red and scratched the top of his head with his long tentacle.

"You've never heard of Koa? He was the best friend of the first chief of our island, Chief Kealohi, hundreds of years ago. It all started one night when the chief was stargazing from his canoe. An enormous whale jumped out of the water, and accidently knocked him off the canoe. Chief Kealohi plunged down into the dark sea. The whale swam beneath him, offering his giant fin to bring him to the surface. The chief clung tight to the fin and rode the sea giant all the way to the top. The whale saved his life. They became best friends from that moment on. The chief named the whale Koa, after the strong Koa wood on our island."

Celeste asked, "What about the pearl?"

"Right! Well, the next night Chief Kealohi, paddled his canoe out to sea to stargaze. Koa rose slowly from below the sea, taking great care not to tip the canoe over. In his mouth, the whale carried a large purple pearl and gave it to the chief. It was Chief Kealohi's most valuable possession and he wore it around his neck at all times. He called it the Kalani Pearl, meaning sky pearl, because it held all the colors of the sky. The pearl became a symbol of friendship between them and represents the bond between man and whale. Without the Kalani Pearl, the sea giants won't return to Ka La'ume Bay."

Celeste's eyes widened. "They won't return to the island without it?"

"Nope. That's why I'm protecting it with my life."

My best friend Mya is a sea giant. She has to return! I haven't seen her in almost six full moons."

She blew a large air bubble and twirled her nose around it, forming the bubble into the shape of a young whale.

"Cute kid. Tell me something…why are you here? Why aren't you helping your mother with the preparations of the welcome ceremony?"

Celeste gulped, and the air bubble popped. "You know my mother?"

"Of course, I do. You're Naomi's kid. Her job is just as important as mine. Most dolphins your age would dive at the chance to help out with the ceremony, especially if their best friend…was a sea giant."

Celeste's heart felt like it sank down to her tail.

"I was actually on my way to help her when I saw the lantern fish," Celeste tried to explain but Ollie just stared at her with his golden eyes.

"Well…I guess I'd better get going then."

"You do that. See ya around kid." Ollie began to fade.

"It was nice meeting you," she said, but she could no longer see him. She swam as fast as she could to help her mother.

CHAPTER 4

THE JOURNEY NORTH

Celeste spent the rest of the afternoon helping her mother. She worked harder than she had ever worked before. She braided seaweed, gathered coral, and learned how to string seashells into beautiful necklaces. Using seaweed as the rope, she and the other dolphins created a mile-long pathway for the sea giants to swim down. They lined the edges of the path with floating flowers and tropical leaves. Everything was set in place and her mother seemed pleased, but the dolphin elders commented on how dark the path was. This gave Celeste an idea! She thought of asking the lantern fish if they could help light up the path during the ceremony. But the day had come to an end, and she would have to ask them the next day.

Celeste looked out to the horizon, where the ocean ended and connected to the sky. The sun slowly plunged below the sea like a lazy eye closing to dream of tomorrow. Soon, both sea and sky blended together into one dark blanket. Millions of stars above her reflected onto the water and it appeared as if she was drifting in space, surrounded completely by stars. The soft glow of the moon shone down on the slow waves that surrounded her and moved like a cape in the wind. She floated and wondered when her best friend Mya would return.

"Tired, little one?" Celeste's mother nuzzled in closer.

"Not that much." whispered Celeste in a sleepy voice, trying to keep her eyes open.

"Well, you should be. You worked hard this afternoon. I'm very proud of you."

"I should have been helping you sooner. I'm so sorry, mama."

"I forgive you. There will be plenty of work to be done tomorrow. I'm counting on you to help."

"Yes mama."

"Ollie told me you paid him a visit today?" Her mother glared down at Celeste who avoided her stare.

"Yup." Celeste cringed because she knew she was in trouble for swimming beyond the coral reef.

"He also told me you were a brave little dolphin and tried to help the lantern fish."

Celeste froze. Her mother continued, "I'm proud of you, but you could've gotten hurt. I've warned you about swimming past the coral reefs."

"I know mama, I'm sorry." Celeste yawned and fought to keep her eyes open. "Ollie started telling me the tale of the Great Whale Star. But I still don't understand why the sea giants leave the island each year."

Her mother smiled, "Are you sure you're not too sleepy to hear the tale?"

Celeste yawned, "Nope."

They both looked up to the starry sky, as her mother began telling her the tale.

"Koa and Chief Kealohi became best friends, helping each other over the years. Koa ruled under the sea, Kealohi ruled over the island. When lighting struck the island, and a fire destroyed the village's crops, it was Koa and his kind who provided fish to the people until the next harvest. One summer, when the sun heated the waters to a temperature too hot for the whales, Chief Kealohi suggested Koa guide his kind to the cooler waters of the North."

"He told him, 'Jump high and swallow the brightest star in the northern sky. It will guide you to cooler waters. When winter approaches, return home to warm waters of Ka La'ume Bay.'"

"Koa agreed but wondered how they would find their way home. The chief assured him, 'For hundreds of years, the ocean has given us rare, purple pearls. After the fourth full moon, we will gather them, crush them into a fine sand, and toss their dust into the morning clouds. Each morning when the sun rises to kiss the clouds, the pearls' colors will be painted across the sky, and you will know the way to your homeland.'"

"And it has been this way for hundreds of years," her mother finished.

Celeste, still fighting off her sleepiness, stared up into the star-lit sky. She remembered seeing the people of the village crushing the pearls into large bowls, the chief standing on the highest cliff, and tossing pearl dust into the clouds. She was grateful knowing they were helping her best friend Mya return home.

When Celeste couldn't fight the heaviness of sleep any longer, she slept the way all dolphins sleep: she closed one eye, leaving the other one open, and drifted off to sleep.

CHAPTER 5

THE GREAT WHALE STAR

The next morning, Celeste woke to the sound of sea gulls flying by, then swam to her mother who was making leis for the ceremony.

"Are they here yet?"

"Good morning sleepyhead, no, not yet. Any day now." Her mother caressed her. "I need you to help me make leis today. I think it would be wonderful if you made one for Mya."

Celeste loved the idea of making her best friend a special welcome gift and spent a good part of the morning helping her mother make leis out of seaweed, sea shells, and coral.

Celeste asked, "Why do they call Koa the Great Whale Star?"

"Well, you fell asleep last night before I could tell you the rest of the tale. I can finish it now, if you'd like?"

"Yes, please!"

"Eventually, Koa and the chief grew very old, but they never missed a night of stargazing together. One evening, Koa told his friend, 'My heart is old and weak, and I believe my death is near. What will happen to my kind if I can no longer guide them to the North?'"

"When the chief heard his friend's concern, he asked the Creator of the Sea, and Stars, and Sky to take Koa's spirit and place him among the sea of stars forever. It was the only way he could continue guiding his kind to the northern seas."

"That night, Koa swam to shore. The people of the village sang songs of friendship and gratitude to him. They draped braided seaweed, intertwined with flowers, long strands of red coral, pink shells and purple pearls, across Koa's body."

"When it was time, Koa took his last breath, and like a gust of cold wind from the North, he exhaled thousands of northern stars he had swallowed from all of his migrating journeys. The stars drifted to the sky and formed a Great Whale Star."

"Koa yelled down to the chief, 'For as long as the stars shine in the night's sky, you will always be my friend.'"

"The chief yelled up to his friend, 'For as long as the sun rises to kiss the clouds, you will always be my friend.' Then the whale swam away into the darkness of the sky. And that night, the chief took the Kalani Pearl necklace from around his neck and tossed it back into the sea."

"The chief told the people on the island, and the creatures of the sea, 'My gratitude to the ocean is endless, for out of the sea came the greatest friendship of my lifetime. It is here, where the Kalani Pearl must be hidden and well protected. Each year, when the sea giants return from the northern seas, the pearl will be retrieved from the depths of the ocean and worn as a promise of friendship between man and whale.'"

"Then the chief took his last breath, and like a warm wind off Ka La'ume Bay, he exhaled a brilliant star that rose above the island."

Celeste's mother finished with, "For hundreds of years, the Kalani Pearl is worn during the ceremony to welcome the sea giants home."

Celeste finished braiding the lei for Mya and couldn't wait to give it to her. She wanted Mya's return to be spectacular. She overheard her mother and the dolphin elders discussing the decorated path being too dark.

"Mama, I have an idea. I'll be right back."

"Celeste, you can't leave, you promised to help."

"Mama, you've got to trust me. I won't let you down, I promise." Celeste waited for her mother's response.

Her mother paused for a moment, then agreed, "Fine." Then she tossed her a net, "Grab some more coral on your way back... and be careful!"

Celeste hooked the net to her tail and swam as fast as she could through the tall kelp forest. No sign of the lantern fish. She peeked over the coral reef, but there was no sign of them there either. There was only one place they could be: Ollie's home, the abandoned ship! But his home was beyond the coral reefs, and she didn't want to disobey her mother again.

Just then, she heard a scuffle and loud grunts coming from the ship. She heard it again and she knew something was wrong. If Ollie was in trouble, she had to help him! She swam close to the dark hole of the ship and peeked her head in. She could hear fumbling and rumbling sounds, but she couldn't see a thing. The lantern fish were gone, and it was very dark, except for a single blue light in the corner of the ceiling of the ship. She snuck in through the hole trying not to be seen and swam towards the blue light. It was one little lantern fish, hiding behind a wooden beam.

"Sorry little guy, I hate to do this to you, but it's for Ollie." She swooped the little fish into her mouth and held him between her teeth, using him like a flashlight. He squirmed and wiggled, but she wasn't about to let him go.

She shined the light in the middle of the ship and there they were! Ollie and Hewa battling it out! The wooden cart was tipped over and the Kalani Pearl was gone! She searched the floor for the pearl. Nothing. She noticed the eel held something in his mouth. It was the pearl! Ollie squeezed his arms tight around the eel, who twisted and flipped trying to escape.

She remembered what Ollie told her: *without the Kalani Pearl, the sea giants won't return.* She thought of the friendship between Koa and Chief Kealohi, and the sea giants returning home with her best friend Mya. There was no way she was going to let Hewa get away with the Kalani Pearl!

Celeste felt a surge of fire rush through her body and build up in her tail. She swam toward the eel and slugged him with her tail. *WHACK!* The pearl dropped and began slowly descending into the darkness.

CHAPTER 6

THE RUNNER

She spun around and saw the eel's jaw snapping towards her! Ollie grabbed him by the neck with his long tentacle and yanked him away.

"Get the pearl!" Ollie shouted at Celeste.

Without a second to spare, Celeste rushed towards the pearl, dropped the little lantern fish, and caught the pearl in her mouth.

"Go kid, go! Take the pearl to the elders!" Ollie ordered as he struggled with the eel. Celeste headed for the opening of the ship. But just then, she heard a gut-wrenching scream echo through the ship as Hewa bit off one of Ollie's tentacles. Blue blood oozed everywhere.

Celeste stopped and began swimming back to help him.

"No! Save the pearl!" Ollie yelled at her.

Celeste hesitated for a second, but then got an idea. With the Kalani Pearl held tight in her mouth, and the net hooked on her tail, she swam as fast as she could straight towards the eel. He took the challenge and chuckled at her attempt, swimming towards her. He opened his mouth and she stared deep into his red eyes. Just as she was a foot away from him, she took a sharp turn upwards, swimming towards the ceiling of the ship. Hewa swam right into the net hooked on her tail and became entangled in it! The more he squirmed and struggled, the more entrapped he became. Celeste whipped around, and quickly exited the ship with Hewa squirming in the net behind her. She knew she had to swim fast if this plan was going to work! She didn't stop and bolted towards the surface of the water. She could see rays of sun beaming through the water, and she knew she was almost there. She thought of Koa, jumping high into the sky to swallow the brightest northern star! She shot straight out of the water like a rocket, then came crashing down, whipping the net hard against the water. The eel was knocked out cold.

Ollie surfaced, "Nice work kid! I'll take it from here." He grabbed the Kalani Pearl from her mouth with one of his tentacles.

"Ollie! You're alive!" Celeste exclaimed, "There was blue blood everywhere! I thought you were dead!"

"Nah, it's just an arm. It'll grow back," he assured her as he took the net with the eel inside. "Mmmm, grumpy eel…my favorite." He chuckled. "Thanks kid!"

Celeste's mother and the elders saw the commotion and rushed over.

"What's happened? Everything okay?" her mother asked.

"Naomi, this kid of yours…"

"Yes?" Celeste's mother held her breath, and gritted her teeth, as the elders watched.

"She's amazing! She just saved the Kalani Pearl from being stolen!"

The crowd gasped and cheered.

"Tell me one thing kid, why'd you do it?"

"Do what?"

"I told you to save the Kalani Pearl, but you came back to help me. Why?"

"Well, the Kalani Pearl represents Koa and Chief Kealonhi's friendship, and well, I'd like to think you're my friend, Ollie."

Ollie smiled, "Aw, gee. Thanks kid. Then my decision is made."

He turned to the gathered sea creatures and exclaimed, "As Keeper of the Kalani Pearl this year, I choose Celeste as this year's Runner!"

Everyone cheered, and Celeste's mother gleamed with pride.

"Runner? What's a—" Celeste tried to ask, but Ollie quickly wrapped his tentacle around her mouth, preventing her from speaking.

"Quiet kid, you'll ruin the moment. Just smile and take it all in. I'll explain everything to you later."

CHAPTER 7

THE RETURN OF THE SEA GIANTS

Later that night, the cold winds blew in from the north, and with it, a brilliant cluster of stars in the shape of a gigantic whale came crashing through. Stars scattered and sprayed like waves of water as his enormous body swam through them. The starlit beast dove straight down, plummeting towards the ocean, then just before he touched the sea, he curved and shot upwards. His tail was so massive that he shoved the moon clear across the sky when he swam past it. He swam closer towards the bay and peered down to the island. People on the island stood in awe, and sea creatures of all kinds popped their heads out from the water to see the magnificent being. And little Celeste... well, she was sound asleep!

"Celeste..." his faint voice echoed through the wind on the waves.

Celeste woke and saw a million stars falling from the sky, like rain, sinking into the dark sea and disappearing like the sun sinks into the horizon each night.

"Celeste," came his rumbling voice again, this time louder, like thunder.

She quivered when she saw the majestic beast swimming above her.

Celeste gasped. "You're Koa, the Great Whale Star!"

"I am," he said, and when his deep voice sounded, it caused the water around her to ripple, "and you are Celeste, the brave young dolphin who helped defend the Kalani Pearl."

Celeste nodded as her eyes widened, "I am."

"Thank you, little one." Then he rumbled loudly for all to hear, "From the North, and across the horizon, we swam. Another long journey from the cold northern seas has come to an end, never ceasing until we reached the tropical waters of our beloved homeland. Home of our life-long friends, the island of the purple pearl, and painted sky…the safe place of our sacred Kalani Pearl! Alas, the sea giants of Ka La'ume Bay have returned! Let! The! Ceremony! Begin!" Koa jumped high and splashed into a cluster of stars that flung across the sky like firecrackers.

The young chief of the island, who was standing tall in his canoe, turned and signaled to his people on land. With their fire torches, they ignited a long path of fire that ran along the beach. The chief blew a conch shell to the North, then East, South and West. The people of the village pounded heavy, deep drums, as dancers swayed their hips and sang and shook feathered rattles in their hands.

Ollie instructed Celeste, "Okay kid, you know what to do, right?" He placed the Kalani Pearl braided tight in seaweed around her neck.

Celeste nodded, "Yes!"

"Go! Swim fast! And don't forget the flips," Ollie coached.

"Got it!"

Celeste swam down the middle of the long pathway towards the chief, as the lantern fish followed her, lighting up the pathway and sparkling like stars. When she reached the halfway mark, she jumped out of the water and double flipped! Then thrust forward with a powerful push and double flipped again!

"Ooooo! Ahhhh!" Everyone cheered.

Ollie was pleased. "Nice job kid," he whispered under his breath.

After swimming the entire path, she reached the edge of the chief's canoe. She lowered her head with respect, just as Ollie instructed her to do.

The chief smiled down at her and said, "Mahalo, nai'a," which means "thank you, dolphin." Then he reached down gently and stroked her head. He took the Kalani Pearl necklace from around her neck and replaced it with a lei made of flowers. He stood up and yelled, "Koa, Great Whale Star, as long as the sun rises to kiss the clouds, we will always be friends!"

Then Koa shouted down to the chief, "As long as the stars shine in the night's sky, we will always be friends!"

As the ceremony continued, Celeste kept her eyes on the horizon, patiently waiting for Mya. Then far in the distance, where the night's sky meets the blackness of the ocean, they came, one by one. She could see the moonlight on their sleek dark bodies. They plunged down into the dark water, disappearing from sight, before thrusting their enormous bodies out of the water, and crashing down onto the sea waves.

Then finally, Celeste saw a glimpse, between the gigantic bodies that surrounded her, of her friend Mya, the youngest of the Sea Giants.

"There she is! Mya!" she yelled, as she watched her swim down the lit up pathway.

"Mya!" She yelled again and darted through the water carrying the braided lei she made her.

"Celeste!" Mya shouted to her as they swam faster towards each other. Celeste flipped and twirled around Mya, then playfully bumped her nose against her forehead.

Mya flipped and rolled with excitement, "I'm home! I'm finally home!"

"You're here! Welcome back!" Celeste placed the lei around Mya's neck. "I made this for you."

"Thank you, this is beautiful! I have something for you too." Mya gave her a jade spiral stone that hung from strands of seaweed, "It's a jade stone, from the northern seas. It's supposed to bring you good luck."

"It's beautiful! I love it! Thank you!"

While the ceremony continued, the two swam around the island, chatting and swapping stories of their adventures. Eventually, the ceremony came to an end. Celeste glanced up to the sky and saw Koa swimming away towards the brightest star far above the island.

"Where's he going?" Celeste asked.

"Each night, he visits his old friend, Chief Kealohi, the brightest star above the island. They've been friends forever…just like us."

Celeste looked at her jade stone necklace and said, "For as long as the sun rises to kiss the clouds, and the stars shine in the night's sky, we will always be friends."

~The End~

ABOUT THE AUTHOR

Toria Hungerford has been writing creatively since childhood. She wrote this book after wondering how whales migrated each winter without getting lost. She says, "I imagined they followed the stars as a map, and that is how The Great Whale Star, came to be. It was important to write a story reflecting the wise indigenous ways of our ancestors globally, respecting and honoring Mother Nature, as well as loving and protecting it."

Toria lives in Arizona with her husband and three dogs where she spends most of her time submerged in nature and doing what she loves most; writing.

www.ToriaHungerford.com

ABOUT THE ILLUSTRATOR

Aaron Herrera is a professional artist and designer based out of New Mexico. As the creative director and owner of his own design studio, he provides a variety of design media. Visit www.AaronHerrera.com for more information.

26258538R00029

Made in the USA
San Bernardino, CA
17 February 2019